Bogota Public Library
375 Larch Avenue
Bogota, NJ 07603

4/15

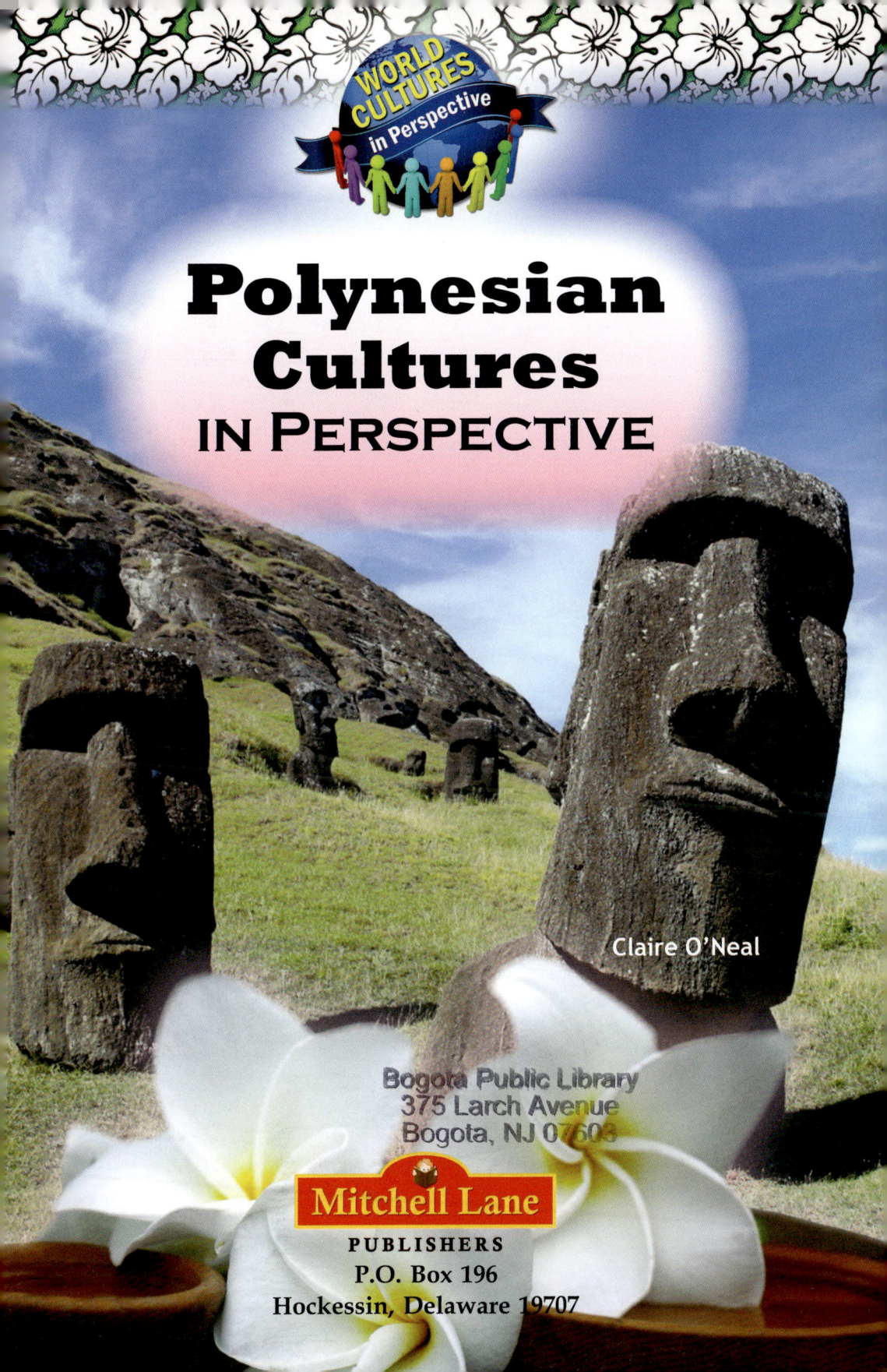

Brazilian Cultures IN PERSPECTIVE

Caribbean Cultures IN PERSPECTIVE

East Asian Cultures IN PERSPECTIVE

Islamic Culture IN PERSPECTIVE

Israeli Culture IN PERSPECTIVE

Louisiana Creole & Cajun Cultures IN PERSPECTIVE

Native Alaskan Cultures IN PERSPECTIVE

North African Cultures IN PERSPECTIVE

Polynesian Cultures IN PERSPECTIVE

Southeast Asian Cultures IN PERSPECTIVE

Copyright © 2015 by Mitchell Lane Publishers, Inc. All rights reserved. No part of this book may be reproduced without written permission from the publisher. Printed and bound in the United States of America.

Printing   1   2   3   4   5   6   7   8   9

Library of Congress Cataloging-in-Publication Data
O'Neal, Claire.
 Polynesian cultures in perspective / by Claire O'Neal.
     pages cm. — (World cultures in perspective)
 Includes bibliographical references and index.
 ISBN 978-1-61228-563-4 (library bound)
 1. Polynesia—Juvenile literature. 2. Polynesia—Social life and customs—Juvenile literature. I. Title.
 DU510.O64 2014
 996—dc23
                                                        2014020461

eBook ISBN: 9781612286020

PUBLISHER'S NOTE: This story is based on the author's extensive research, which she believes to be accurate. Documentation of this research is on pages 60–61.

    The Internet sites referenced herein were active as of the publication date. Due to the fleeting nature of some web sites, we cannot guarantee they will all be active when you are reading this book.

    To reflect current usage, we have chosen to use the secular era designations BCE ("before the common era") and CE ("of the common era") instead of the traditional designations BC ("before Christ") and AD (*anno Domini,* "in the year of the Lord").

PBP

CONTENTS

Introduction: Welcome to Polynesia 6
Chapter 1: WHERE IS POLYNESIA? 8
    Can Polynesia Survive Climate Change? 14
Chapter 2: HAWAIKI, HOMELAND OF
    THE ANCIENT POLYNESIANS 16
    Thor Heyerdahl and the *Kon-Tiki* Expedition 20
Chapter 3: HAOLE: OUTSIDERS COME TO PARADISE 22
    Easter Island (Rapa Nui) and Pitcairn Island 30
Chapter 4: KAHIKO, TRADITION:
    FAMILY, FOOD, AND FAITH 32
    The Coconut 38
Chapter 5: SHARING STORIES: LANGUAGE AND FILM 40
    Aloha! Talofa! Ia Ora Na! Kia Ora! Malo e Lelei 44
Chapter 6: HO ʻOHAUʻOLI: HAVE FUN WITH
    MUSIC, ART, AND SPORTS 46
    Recipe: Po'e (Tahitian Fruit and Coconut Custard) 53
Experiencing Polynesian Culture in the United States 54
Map of Polynesia 57
Chapter Notes 58
Further Reading 60
    Books 60
    Movies 60
    On the Internet 60
    Works Consulted 60
Glossary 62
Index 62

Introduction
Welcome to Polynesia

Palm trees sway in the gentle tradewind breeze. Tides tug on the crystal-clear waters of lagoons, revealing a quiet rainbow of fish and coral. The sun sets over an ancient volcano, now sleeping and blanketed by green forests and waterfalls. As the moon rises and the stars shine bright, age-old stories are shared by firelight. Ancient explorers told the same ones as they sailed here on handmade canoes, their path lit by the stars. Welcome to *Hawaiki*—welcome home. Welcome to Polynesia, where beautiful tropical islands dot the ocean like flowers on a *lei*.

Chances are you are *haole*—an outsider. In some ways, everyone is. Most of the islands of the Pacific lay undiscovered until 1500 BCE, when a great civilization first began to spread out and populate the ocean triangle between Hawaii, New Zealand, and Easter Island. At first, it was an isolated life. Polynesians crafted homes, clothes, and food using only the land and the plants around them. Though the work was hard, the rewards were rich. Polynesians turned the deep magic of nature into spellbinding stories, music, dance, and art.

Passed down through big, close-knit families over the years, the Polynesian spirit of exploration continues. Some Polynesians stay on their island home to encourage modern-day explorers—vacationing haole who come to take in the world's most beautiful scenery. But many Polynesians continue the work their ancestors began. They leave their island home and spread out, creating new islands of culture within other countries, especially New Zealand, Australia, and the United States. We share a little of Polynesia when we dance a hula, cook with coconut or vanilla, gaze at a tattoo, or wonder at mysterious *tiki* god statues. So relax. *Haere maru*— take it slow. Explore the past, present, and future of the people of Polynesia, and their home in paradise on Earth.

Chapter One
Where Is Polynesia?

Legend has it that Maui, the tricky man-god of Polynesian mythology, made a fishhook from a magical jawbone. When he was far out to sea, Maui threw his line over the side of his canoe, chanting a powerful spell. The hook dropped deeper and deeper under the water until Maui felt a tug. He tugged back—it was a whopper!—and gently coaxed his catch to the surface. Turns out Maui's "fish" was a whole island!

Maui must have been quite the fisherman. Thousands of small, often far-flung islands in the Pacific are together known as Oceania. Geographers divide up Oceania into three groups of islands. Micronesia contains the northwest-most grouping of islands. Greek for "small islands," Micronesia includes the Marshall Islands, the Mariana Islands (including Guam), Wake Island, and the Republics of Palau and Nauru. Melanesia contains the southwest group of islands, and also the most land of the three groups. Greek for "black islands," Melanesia includes Papua New Guinea, the Solomon Islands, Vanuatu, and Fiji.

Polynesia, Greek for "many islands," covers a much larger region of the Pacific Ocean than the other two groups (see map on page 57). Polynesia is not a single country or area, but rather a name for the triangle of area in the Pacific Ocean formed by Hawaii, Easter Island, and New Zealand. Each side of this triangle spans over 4,000 miles (6,400 kilometers), enclosing an area more than twice the size of the continental United States. Most of this territory is empty ocean, but more than one thousand islands lay sprinkled throughout this tropical region.

On the clusters of islands that have land to farm and supplies of fresh water, Polynesians built their nations. Take a tour of these nations and island groups from west to east, following along on the map on page 57.

The nation of Tuvalu (population 10,782) lies alone in the far west, made up of nine atolls. The two main islands of Samoa (pop. 196,628) are Upolu and Savai'i. The latter of the two, at 656 square miles (1,700 square kilometers), is one of the largest islands in Polynesia. American Samoa (pop. 54,517), a US territory, claims the eastern islands of the Samoan chain. People of the Kingdom of Tonga (pop. 106,440) live on forty islands; more than one hundred of Tonga's other islands are uninhabited.[1] The Cook Islands (pop. 10,134) are made up of fifteen small islands, while Niue (pop. 1,190) claims just one. Both are independent nations supported by New Zealand for protection and representation in foreign affairs. The groups once known as the Society Islands (including Tahiti), the Marquesas Islands, the Austral Islands, and the Tuamotu Archipelago are all overseas collectivities of France, known today as French Polynesia (pop. 280,026). Hawaii (pop. 1,404,054), an island chain and a US state, marks the triangle's northern tip. The nation of New Zealand (pop. 4,401,916) forms the triangle's southern tip, while the Pitcairn Islands (pop. 48) and Easter Island (pop. 5,761) make up Polynesia's most eastern points.[2]

Geology

Ancient Hawaiians told the myth of Pele to make sense of the island chain's active and frightening geology. Beautiful and fierce,

Chapter One

they said, Hawaii's fire goddess Pele makes her home inside Mount Kilauea, Hawaii, one of the most active volcanoes on Earth. The lava that cooled on its slopes forms her long, black hair. Volcanoes erupt when she digs into the ground with her *pa'oe*, or magic stick. Earthquakes rock the Pacific when she stamps her feet in rage. Pele's story is partly true—sea floor volcanoes have slowly built many of Polynesia's islands, stacking layer upon layer of cooled lava over time. Hawaii's Mauna Loa, measured from its base deep underwater to its crater, stands 30,085 feet (9,170 meters)—taller than Mount Everest! Hawaiian volcanoes like Kilauea and Mauna Loa erupt gently and frequently. But sometimes Pele surprises the islanders. Tonga's undersea volcano Hunga Tonga-Hunga Ha'apai erupted so violently in 2009 that it spewed rock and ash into the sky and killed all of the plants and animals on the nearby island of Hunga Ha'apai.

Luckily, most of Polynesia's volcanoes are extinct and aging gracefully. The wet warmth of tropical rains breaks down ash and lava to create some of the most fertile soils on Earth. Rainbows of colorful wild fruit and flowers decorate Tonga, Samoa, the

Mauna Loa has been erupting for the last seven hundred thousand years. Its lava flows helped to build the island of Hawaii.

Where Is Polynesia?

Marquesas Islands, Hawaii, and the Pitcairn Islands as crystal waterfalls carve through deep green forests. Water and wind eventually wear down these fire-born mountains completely, at least the ones which have not sunk beneath the waves because of movements in the Earth's crust.

The undersea walls of volcanoes create the perfect nursery for marine life. Corals busily build reefs higher and higher to create circular atolls which often remain above the ocean's surface after the tops of the volcanoes they surround sink back underwater. The Cook Islands atolls host lush fish populations, making them popular with scuba divers. The island of Niue is also made of coral, but shifts in the earth's crust raised it higher than other Polynesian atolls. The low-lying Tuamotu Archipelago in French Polynesia forms the largest chain of atolls in the world. The Tuamotus spread seventy-seven atolls out over the Pacific Ocean to cover an area the size of Western Europe, but only represent 310 square miles (800 square kilometers) of land.[3] Sailors know and fear the Tuamotus as the "Dangerous Archipelago" from the many shipwrecks caused

> The warm, crystal clear waters of Aitutaki in the Cook Islands make it a snorkeling paradise. Divers can swim among the rainbow coral with eels, turtles, rays, and colorful fish.

Chapter One

by the hidden, sharp reefs. But despite the beauty of their blue-green lagoons and abundant seafood to catch, most atolls do not support human habitats. They have little soil to farm, and sometimes no fresh water.

Climate

Most islands in Polynesia lie within the tropics. The islands bask in warm daily temperatures, averaging 70° to 80°F (21° to 27°C) year-round, and over 60 inches (1500 millimeters) of rainfall annually.[4] Polynesians divide their year into two seasons. The traditional Season of Plenty—the southern-hemisphere "summer"—begins on November 20 each year, when the constellation Pleiades rises above the horizon at night. Ancient Polynesians knew that Pleiades, or *Matari'i*, would bring abundant rain to help crops grow. Many islands hold festivals between February and mid-June to celebrate

Cyclone Oli hit Polynesia in February 2010. On Tubuai Island in French Polynesia, the damaging wind and waves were even strong enough to pick up cars.

the harvests.⁵ But occasionally, typhoons and cyclones that can strike between January and March destroy whole towns, or contaminate an island's drinking water with ocean salt. The Season of Scarcity begins on May 20, when Matari'i drops out of sight and takes the rain with it. Today, "Scarcity" hardly describes it—the drier season brings tourists and their money during the Northern Hemisphere's summer vacation.

New Zealand presents a very different picture of Polynesia than the typical sandy-beach postcard. First, New Zealand's islands are bigger—the South Island (58,084 square miles, or 150,437 square kilometers) and the North Island (43,911 square miles, or 113,729 square kilometers) are each over ten times larger than the next-largest Polynesian island, the main island of Hawaii. Second, even the North Island of New Zealand lies too far south to grow important Polynesian plants like coconut palms. New Zealand experiences four seasons, including cold, snowy winters on the South Island. In fact, the South Island serves as a home for penguins, and a home base for scientists studying Antarctica.

Yellow-eyed penguin, The Catlins, New Zealand

Can Polynesia Survive Climate Change?

South Pacific islanders live on the front lines in Earth's war against global warming. Increased carbon dioxide in the air changes the chemistry of the oceans, killing off native Polynesian marine animals like corals and oysters. Climate change also threatens the Polynesian way of life with extinction. Scientists predict that world ocean levels will rise at least 30 inches, and as much as 72 inches, (76 to 183 centimeters) by the year 2100.[6] In French Polynesia, the Cook Islands, Niue, and Tonga, the rising tide and ocean storms combine to swallow up farms and businesses near the shore. When the entire population lives on a flat atoll, like Tuvalu, Tokelau, or Hawaii's Midway and Laysan, ocean salt water can easily pollute the fresh water used for drinking. These islanders may soon be forced to abandon their homelands in favor of higher ground.

Vava'u, Tonga

For now, Polynesians choose to stay and fight by adopting alternative energy. The tiny, three-island New Zealand territory of Tokelau is today completely powered by solar panels, which are backed up by generators that run on coconut biofuel.[7] Tonga, on the other hand, took its first step towards renewable energy in 2013 when the nation's first wind turbine began to provide energy.[8] But islanders cannot stem the tide alone. Tuvalu's former prime minister, Maatia Toafa, shares that his nation has already seen the effects of climate change firsthand—coastal erosion, coral bleaching, and an increase in severe storms are among the islands' problems today. If the warming trend continues, Polynesia will disappear beneath the waves.[9]

Chapter Two
Hawaiki, Homeland of the Ancient Polynesians

In the beginning there was only father Rangi and mother Papa. Like two halves of a clamshell, they lay locked together, embraced for all time. From their love grew many sons. But the sons grew up trapped between Rangi and Papa and yearned to break free. One day, son Tane lay on his back like the roots of a tree. With his strong legs, he pushed Rangi up to become the sky, and with his head, he pushed Papa down to become the earth. The sky and earth have remained apart ever since, held up by forest-god Tane's tall trees. Rangi still cries for his wife each night, his tears of dew left behind for her in the morning. Sometimes Papa heaves herself upward, blasting the earth to the sky, but still they stay apart.

Like Papa and Rangi's sons, the Lapita people suffered from overcrowding in their original homeland in what is today northern Papua New Guinea. Around 1500 BCE, a few adventurous Lapita families set sail for the unknown in handmade canoes. These expert navigators found their way by noticing patterns in the waves and wind and clouds. By day, they followed routes taken by birds and fish. Constellations, especially the Southern Cross, guided them at night. The wind and water fought them nearly the entire way, since the currents of the Pacific waters and Polynesian breezes flow from east to west.[1] The Lapita also weathered storms and typhoons, with waves big enough to topple their small boats right into the shark-infested waters. After days, weeks, or even months at sea on a journey of over one thousand miles, not all sailors would survive.

Those who did became the first humans on Polynesia. They created a new Hawaiki, or homeland, on the white sands of Tonga and Samoa. They found rich soil, seafood like crab and tuna, and, most importantly, fresh water from inland lakes and streams. The Lapita also brought important food crops with them—the potato-like taro (TAHR-oh) root; starchy, plentiful breadfruit; rich, sweet tropical fruits like banana; and especially coconut. They brought pigs and dogs to raise as pets and food. They built *fale*—sturdy log huts constructed on raised stone platforms—and formed small villages centered around farming or fishing.

Taro grows on a plantation in Hawaii. Taro root is a nutritious, starchy vegetable used in many Polynesian dishes. The leaves and stems can also be eaten when young and tender. Taro must be cooked—it is toxic when raw.

Chapter Two

Some carried on the spirit of adventure. Innovative Polynesians improved their canoes by connecting one or two floats to the boat for added stability. These sturdier canoes may have boasted more storage for longer journeys. Around 200 BCE, a handful of island adventurers used these new boats, called outrigger canoes, to cross the sea once more. They made a new Hawaiki on the Society Islands and the Marquesas Islands, in what is today French Polynesia. Soon, villages of *bure*—lighter-weight bamboo-pole huts with woven grass walls and roofs—sprang up on these beaches and hillsides.

The explorers were ready to sail again by 300 CE. Some sailed southwest to the Cook Islands; others headed southeast to colonize Easter Island. Around 400 CE, sailors pointed their boats north, to Hawaii. And around 900 CE, still others would venture to New Zealand, the last place in Polynesia to be settled by humans.[2]

Polynesians flourished, thanks to a bounty of food harvested in their gentle climate. But island life was not easy. Storms could quickly wipe out crops and cause an entire island population to suffer famine. Polynesian societies developed strict customs and rules to survive. Commoners farmed the land, giving most of their crops and resources to the *ali'i*, or ruler of an island or group of islands. Ancient Polynesians believed that the ali'i's power came from *mana*, a gift from the gods that gave the ali'i the right to rule. Ali'i led warriors into battle against other ali'i. They controlled access to food and other resources. Fair ali'i made sure everyone got their share. But some ali'i treated commoners as slaves. Ali'i in Tahiti and Hawaii even practiced human sacrifice. When their gods demanded, they killed—and sometimes ate—low-status villagers or enemies captured in battle.

For any ali'i to marry, or even be touched by, a commoner was absolutely *tapu*. When something was tapu, it was forbidden—it could not be touched. Things that were tapu were so sacred or holy that they were dangerous for ordinary people. On some islands using Bonito tuna, squid, or turtle for food was tapu. Leaves that provided shade for people were also tapu, not to be harvested. To violate tapu brought the wrath of the gods on you, your family, or your entire island.

Hawaiki, Homeland of the Ancient Polynesians

This fale on a Samoan beach is built in the time-honored and resourceful style of the islands.

Thor Heyerdahl and the *Kon-Tiki* Expedition
Thor Heyerdahl (1914–2002), an anthropologist from Norway, was convinced that Polynesia's first settlers must have come from the coast of Peru. He found that blood types from native Polynesians sometimes matched modern South Americans. He ate sweet potatoes on the Marquesas, knowing that South Americans love them, too, and that both cultures call them *kumara*. Heyerdahl believed that, because wind and water currents in the South Pacific flowed east-to-west, a journey from South America to Easter Island could be as simple as drifting across the Pacific on a raft. Heyerdahl set out to do just that. With a crew of five men, he built a raft, the *Kon-Tiki*, using only traditional materials. Instead of using nails, Heyerdahl lashed balsa wood timbers together with handmade hemp ropes. The *Kon-Tiki* launched from Callao, Peru, on April 28, 1947. The men weathered fierce storms and bloodthirsty sharks. The *Kon-Tiki* drifted for 101 days before landing safely on Raroia Atoll in the Tuamotu Islands. Heyerdahl's account of his voyage became both a best-selling book and an Oscar-winning movie. Though anthropologists later proved Heyerdahl wrong—overwhelming evidence from DNA and ancient artifacts showed that the original Polynesians came from Asia—he may have been at least partly correct. In 2011, Professor Erik Thorsby's tests revealed that some modern Easter Islanders had indigenous South American genes, meaning that at least a few Polynesians intermarried with South Americans in the past.[3]

Chapter Three
Haole: Outsiders Come to Paradise

For most of the world's history, the Polynesian islands lay unnoticed by other world civilizations. Portuguese explorer Ferdinand Magellan was the first haole—outsider—to lay eyes on Polynesia in March 1521. He landed there during the first-ever voyage around the world, from 1519 to 1522. Magellan's funding came from King Philip of Spain, who had hoped to discover a western route to the Spice Islands, in modern-day Indonesia.

The ancient Greek philosopher Aristotle had long ago proposed that a huge continent in the southern hemisphere must exist. With such enormous continents in the northern hemisphere, how else could the planet balance? According to legend, *Terra Australis* might house the wealth of King Solomon of the Bible. Dreams of gold, gems, and spices fueled excitement in Europe for such an adventure. So in November 1567, Spanish explorer Álvaro de Mendaña y Neira set off with an expedition from the coast of Peru in search of the riches of Terra Australis. He spotted the island of Nui in Tuvalu two months into his first voyage. By February, his crew had landed at Santa Isabel Island in the Solomon Islands.

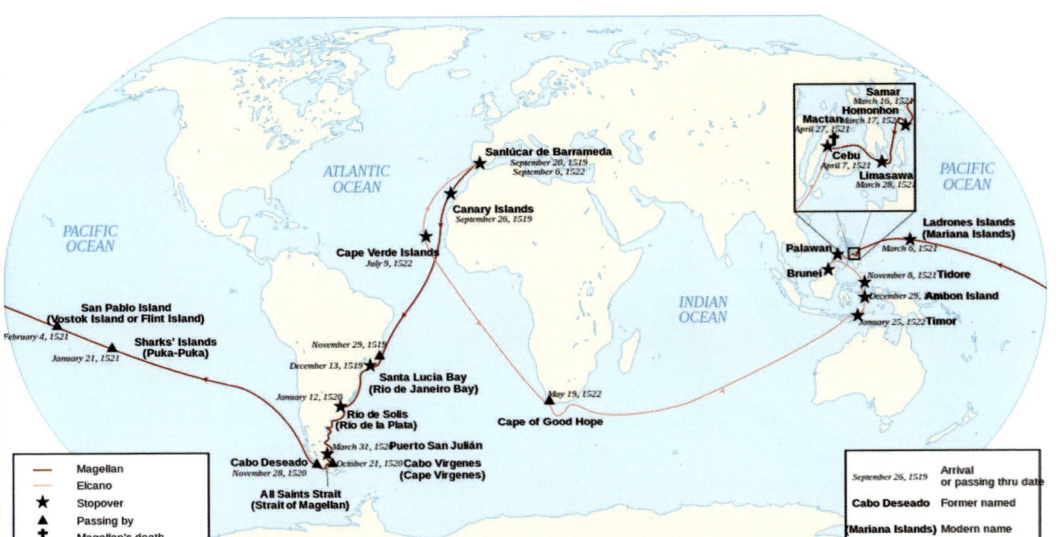

This map charts Magellan's history-making voyage from 1519 to 1522, a trip he himself did not survive. Juan Sebastián Elcano finished the journey from the Philippines, arriving in Spain on the only remaining ship, the *Victoria*.

Mendaña repeated his trip in 1595, and this time made landfall on the Marquesas Islands on July 21. He named this new discovery after the Spanish viceroy, or *marqués*, of Peru.

Mendaña's reports gave the outside world its first glimpse into Polynesian life. Mendaña saw strong warrior men, covered in tattoos from head to toe, fishing from canoes in the still waters. He saw beautiful women, many wearing only loincloths, catching crabs from tide pools.[1] The curious Polynesians saw him, too. Hundreds came out in canoes to greet the guest ships. As was their custom, Polynesians expected their guests to hand over generous offerings to show they had come in peace. The Polynesians boarded the Spanish ship and began taking everything in sight. Shocked, Mendaña and his men attacked. The surprised islanders fought with bone and shell, but the Spanish overwhelmed them with guns and steel. By the time Mendaña left two weeks later, around two hundred islanders had died in the violence.[2]

Chapter Three

Spanish explorer Álvaro de Mendaña y Neira

As European explorers found their way into the South Pacific, many encounters led to confusion, misunderstandings, and bloodshed. Explorers from the Dutch East India Company, Jacob LeMaire and Willem Schouten, visited the Tuamotus and Tonga in 1616, but soon ran for their lives. They offended the Tongan chief by refusing to share the ceremonial *kava* drink with him.³ Famous Dutch explorer Abel Tasman discovered what he called *Nieuw Zeeland* in 1642. He sent a landing party ashore, but the Maori attacked, destroying one of their boats and killing several men. Fellow Dutch explorer Jacob Roggeveen found a friendly reception in western Samoa when he discovered it in 1722, but eastern Samoans attacked and killed his men. Maori tribesmen killed—and ate—French explorer Marc-Joseph Marion du Fresne and twenty-six other settlers in June 1772. The Frenchmen had violated tapu by fishing in Manawaora Bay after some tribesmen had drowned there. In 1777, British Captain James Cook asked his hosts on Tonga about tapu, and introduced the word ("taboo") to the English language. Despite Captain Cook's interest in his Polynesian hosts, he was killed in a battle in Hawaii in 1779.

Spain and the Netherlands soon gave up on Polynesia. Coconuts and warm spices like vanilla transported well, and Tahiti's fresh pearls fetched a nice price at European markets, but the islands were simply too far away, and too hard to find, to be of any real value, especially since Terra Australis and its treasure were never found. Nevertheless, Britain and France sent their own

Haole: Outsiders Come to Paradise

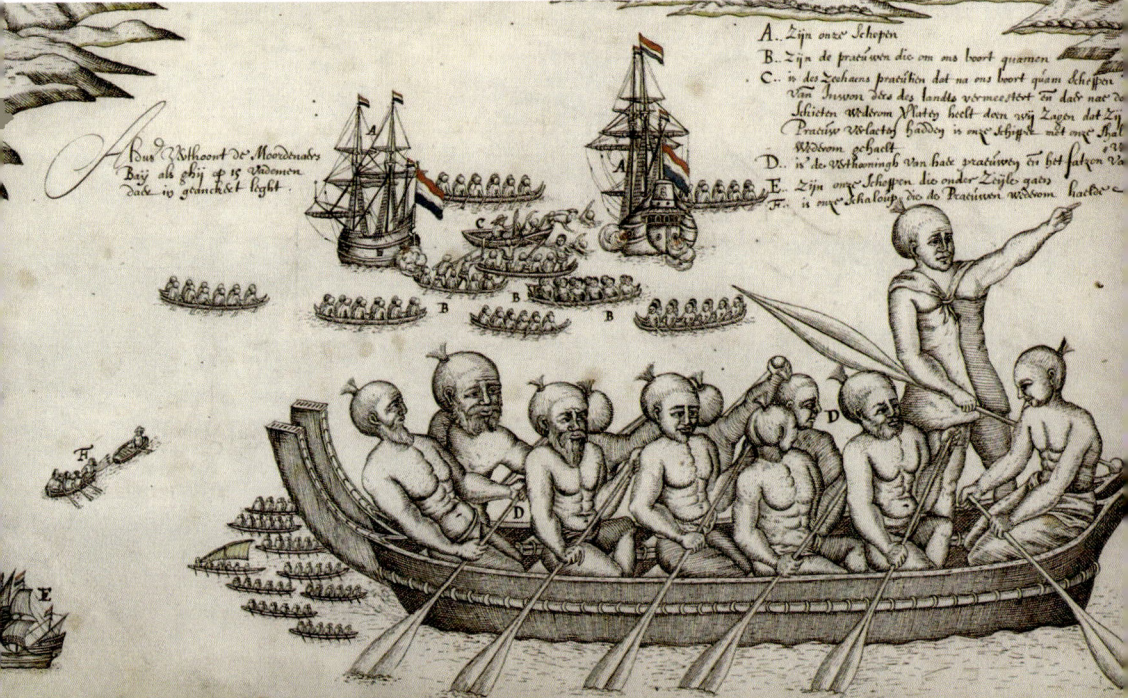

The Maori attacked the Dutch when Abel Tasman anchored his boats in a New Zealand bay in 1642, ramming their canoe into the larger ship. Tasman's artist, Isaack Gilsemans, captured the attack in this picture, becoming the first European to show what the Maori people looked like.

expeditions to the South Pacific. Their reports from Tahiti became the stuff of fantasy.

The sailors on British Captain Samuel Wallis's ship, the HMS *Dolphin*, suffered through hard, long, boring months at sea. They ate nothing but stale or rat-gnawed food. They endured frightening storms and harsh discipline by the captain—whippings or worse—to keep the men from mutiny.[4] In 1767, the *Dolphin* landed on Tahiti. Beautiful women smelling like tropical flowers greeted them on the shore of a warm, aqua-blue lagoon. Their families welcomed the sailors with feasts of coconut and roast pig. They entertained their guests with dancing, singing, and drumming through the

Chapter Three

The Captain James Cook Monument stands inside Kealakekua Bay State Historical Park in Hawaii, commemorating the life and death of the great British explorer.

night. The sailors who arrived exhausted and in pain from their voyage were quickly cured with a delicious diet of bananas and passion fruit picked right off the trees. Tahiti has no metals, so the Polynesians happily traded the sailors wood, fruit, and meat to get tools the islanders would have never seen before, like knives, axes, and nails. One year later, French navigator Louis Antoine de Bougainville and a crew of scientists also sailed to Tahiti, and later Samoa. The strange and wonderful species of Polynesia, from colorful lorikeets to useful spices like vanilla, filled them with awe. De Bougainville returned to France with stories of a people who—to him—seemed free and innocent, knowing nothing else but to eat, make music, and share freely amongst each other, even offering up their beautiful daughters as sailors' brides.

Christian missionaries followed the tales of paradise in search of souls to save. The London Missionary Society set up posts on

Haole: Outsiders Come to Paradise

Tahiti, Tonga, and the Marquesas in 1797, while Americans brought Christianity to Hawaii.[5] French Catholics began working in Tahiti and the Marquesas in the 1830s. The Christians quickly became a powerful influence over ruling families in Polynesia, like Tonga's Chief Taufa'ahau and the Pomare family of Tahiti, convincing the leaders to end their practice of human sacrifice. Missionaries translated the Bible into Polynesian languages, bringing education with them. They built schools and taught island children to read and write in their native language as well as English or French. Though Christians helped in their own way, they had little tolerance for native Polynesian traditions. They frowned upon tattooing. They encouraged Polynesians to wear heavier, hotter, European-style clothes. Ugly and scary tiki gods horrified the missionaries, who destroyed many statues and artifacts. Christians also believed that the wild dancing and music of Polynesia led to sin, and on some islands, outlawed its practice. Many artistic traditions only survived because a handful of Polynesians dared to continue their ancestors' ways in secret.

Foreign powers soon stretched a long arm out to embrace this new, civilized Polynesia. Only the Kingdom of Tonga remained

The 'i'iwi, native to Hawaii

CHAPTER THREE

independent. To this day, Tonga is one of a handful of countries that never became a European colony. France made Tahiti and Tahuata French protectorates in 1842, and later claimed all of the Society Islands, the Marquesas, and the Tuamotus in what is now French Polynesia. In 1893, the United States took over control of Hawaii, removing Queen Lili'uokalani from her throne. Hawaii became a US territory in 1898; one year later, the United States acquired American Samoa from Germany. Britain began with Australia, and in 1788, took on New Zealand. Between 1874 and 1900, Tokelau, the Cook Islands, Tuvalu, and Niue all came under the rule of Britain's Queen Victoria. New, famous settlers chose to stay. Scottish author Robert Louis Stevenson (1850–1894) became a treasured *Tusitala*, or storyteller, to the Samoan people, and even chose to be buried atop Mount Vaea, overlooking Samoa's capital city of Apia.[6] Tahiti inspired French artist Paul Gauguin (1848–1903), who painted rich landscapes and portraits of beautiful Tahitian women.

Paul Gauguin, *Tahitian Landscape* (1891)

Haole: Outsiders Come to Paradise

Outside interest in Polynesia decimated native Polynesian people. European sailors and settlers brought with them influenza, smallpox, tuberculosis, measles, the whooping cough, and many more diseases that ravaged the islanders. Around five hundred thousand Polynesians lived on the Hawaiian islands when they were first discovered by Europe; these deadly new diseases killed off over 90 percent of native Hawaiians in a matter of decades.[7] Stories of the simpleness of Polynesian people also brought slave traders. In the 1860s, ship captains lured Polynesians aboard with promises of a better life abroad. The captains sold those who survived the journey to plantation owners in Peru, Chile, and Australia, or forced them to work in forests or mines. Men and women from Tonga, Samoa, the Cook Islands, Tuvalu, Niue, and Kiribati, and especially from Melanesia and Micronesia, left their homes forever. Many lost their lives. Christian missionaries in Polynesia successfully pleaded with government officials to put a stop to this practice, known as blackbirding.

Colonial ways, both good and bad, continued on many islands through World War II. On December 7, 1941, Japanese warplanes bombed the US naval base in Pearl Harbor, Hawaii. The United States stirred up the calm seas throughout the South Pacific by building airstrips on peaceful islands and atolls like Bora Bora, Rarotonga, Funafuti, and more. The South Pacific islands became the front lines of a war between American and Japanese planes and ships. As World War II ended with Japan's surrender in 1945, world militaries saw a new use for Polynesia. The United States used the Johnston Atoll, Hawaii, as a test site for nuclear bombs between 1958 and 1975. France exploded as many as 180 nuclear weapons on the Moruroa and Fangataufa atolls in the Tuamotus between 1966 and 1996.[8] Though the test sites chosen were uninhabited, the effects of radiation throughout the South Pacific remain a cause for concern. With one voice, Polynesia told the world it had had enough. South Pacific countries signed the Treaty of Rarotonga in 1985. The treaty bans using, testing, or possessing nuclear weapons throughout the South Pacific.

Easter Island (Rapa Nui) and Pitcairn Island

Polynesians first arrived at Easter Island (also known as *Rapa Nui*) in the fourth century. Civilization soon flourished, reaching a peak population of over fifteen thousand by the seventeenth century. Easter Islanders built ceremonial stone platforms, or *ahu*, and the world-famous Easter Island stone statues, the *moai*, to honor their gods. But tribes fought for limited resources on the tiny, crowded island. When Jacob Roggeveen and his band of Dutch sailors first landed on Rapa Nui on Easter Sunday 1722, the island's population had declined to around three thousand people. By the time James Cook arrived in 1774, less than one thousand residents remained—survivors of a changing environment and a violent civil war. The fighting had also toppled the once-proud moai statues. Today, the Easter Island Statue Project works to unearth, restore, and preserve some of the moai, standing them upright once more.[9]

The seven moai of the sacred site of Ahu Akivi on Easter Island

In 1789, British Captain William Bligh insisted it was time for his ship, the HMS *Bounty*, to leave the paradise of Tahiti and set sail for home. Half of his men violently disagreed. Sailor Fletcher Christian led them in a mutiny, kicking Bligh and his eighteen supporters off the ship and leaving them for dead. Realizing that the British Navy would soon be looking for them, Christian decided to search for a place to hide. Sixteen of his men chose to stay in Tahiti, but eight others accompanied him. The mutineers fled with six Tahitian men and eighteen Tahitian women. They landed on the uninhabited Pitcairn Island, and burned the boat to avoid being found. The wreck of the sunken *Bounty* remains underwater there today. By the time an American ship arrived in 1808, all the men except one were dead, though they had left behind more than twenty children from marriages with Tahitian women. Even today, Pitcairn Island's handful of residents mostly descend from the *Bounty's* mutineers. Islanders earn a living by hosting tourists and selling rare Pitcairn Island postage stamps and coins to international collectors.

Chapter Four
Kahiko, Tradition: Family, Food, and Faith

Haere maru—take it slow—relax and enjoy life. This is the unofficial Polynesian motto. Polynesians feel that life's most important things are right in front of them. *Ohana*—family—has always been the heart of Polynesian culture. Families encourage married couples to have lots of children. Parents often share the same house with grandparents and even aunts and uncles. Polynesians feel a strong sense of community that starts with these family bonds. Many spend their free time just hanging out and talking with friends, family, and neighbors. After all, their ancestors had to work together, farming and fishing, to survive.

Food

Polynesians happily use their natural bounty of fresh flavors as an excuse to get together. Island favorites are simple—mix the fruit harvest with freshly caught fish or seafood like yellowfin tuna, eel, crab, lobster, sea urchin, and octopus, or meat like pork or chicken, to make a complete meal. A favorite Hawaiian dish is *poke* (POH-keh), made of raw fish marinated in sea salt and soy sauce. Marquesans and Tahitians prepare a similar delicacy called *fafaru* by placing shrimp in a jar of sea water and allowing it to cook under the sun for a few days. Later, the water is used as a marinade for raw tuna, resulting in a sweet (and smelly) meal.

On Sundays or special occasions, villagers all pitch in to cook a feast in a pit oven dug in dirt or sand. Cooks wrap food in coconut-leaf packets while burning wood preheats the oven. Volcanic rocks placed over the glowing embers serve as a cooking platform and heat source for the food packets. Layers of banana leaves and dirt laid over the pit trap the heat. After a few hours of cooking, the food is dug up, unwrapped, and eaten with the fingers. Each island has its favorite slow-roasted dishes. Samoans love *palusami lu'au*, which is taro—a root like a potato—with coconut cream, wrapped in a taro leaf and cooked. Green bananas

Poke made with ahi tuna

Chapter Four

or breadfruit can be substituted for the taro. Hawaiians celebrating at *luaus* roast a whole pig. *Ono*! (Tasty!)

What could be simpler than picking dessert off the trees in your own backyard? Islanders grow bananas, cassava, mangoes, papayas, passion fruit, pineapple, and citrus fruits in their home gardens. The Polynesian hot dog, a banana sliced longways like a hot dog bun, with coconut slices placed inside, is a favorite Tahitian snack among tourists. Tahiti and other islands grow and export vanilla beans. Hawaii is famous for its pineapple and sugarcane plantations.

A group of Hawaiian tourists gets ready to enjoy an authentic village feast at the Old Lahaina Luau, looking on as their Hawaiian hosts roast a whole pig in an earthen pit.

34

Kahiko, Tradition: Family, Food, and Faith

After dessert, many Hawaiians enjoy a cup of Hawaii's home-grown Kona coffee.

Natural Medicine

To Tongans and Samoans, a shared bowl of kava is as important as a daily cup of coffee. Islanders prepare kava by pulverizing fresh kava root—either by pounding it, grinding it up, or just chewing it and spitting it out—and adding the roots to a bowl of cold water. Friends and family then fill their cups from the bowl and chug the drink immediately. To outsiders, kava tastes like mud. Islanders realize that the taste is unimportant. Kava roots contain medicinal chemicals that help the body to relax. Many countries classify kava as a drug, but Polynesian mothers even use it to soothe their fussy babies.

Breadfruit

Tahiti boasts its own plant-based medicines. French Polynesia's national flower, the *tiare*, or gardenia, produces fragrant, lovely blooms with healing powers. Tahitians crush tiare petals and soak them in coconut oil to make *monoi* oil, used to soften and protect the hair and skin. Tiare-petal medicines can also cure headaches, sunburns, and colds. The *noni*, or Indian mulberry, grows on Tahiti and throughout Polynesia as a large, smelly fruit. Despite its nickname as "the vomit fruit," Polynesians rely on noni to treat health problems ranging from diabetes to stomach and liver diseases. Today, noni extracts and juices are exported from Tahiti and Hawaii to be sold worldwide.

Chapter Four

Ancient Polynesian men and women grew burly and strong on the naturally sweet, fatty diet. But today's hard-working Polynesians typically put in long hours behind a desk instead of hulling a new canoe. Most young Polynesians would rather surf the Internet and play video games than learn the ancient ways of farming and fishing. Obesity is fast becoming a major issue throughout the islands. American Samoa, Samoa, the Cook Islands, Tokelau, Tonga, and Kiribati all have a spot on the list of the world's top ten most obese countries.[1]

Faith

The spirit of Polynesia's history is full of magic and mystery. Whether commoner or ali'i, everyone in an ancient village looked to the priest—known as the *kahuna* in Hawaii, or *tahu'a* in Tahiti—for guidance. The Hawaiian kahuna had important practical powers, like overseeing the construction of a *heiau*, or temple.

Tiki statue, New Zealand

Kahunas studied natural signs to make predictions about the weather or the future. Islanders thought powerful kahunas could use magic to heal, but also to hurt, sending evil spirits to kill an enemy. Polynesians built tiki statues to keep the evil at bay. Tahitian legend tells that the first man was created from red earth and named Ti'i. Tiki stood guard outside important buildings like the *marae*, or sacred meeting house. Tiki still surround and protect important cultural sites, including the marae that still stand throughout the islands.

Kahiko, Tradition: Family, Food, and Faith

Christianity now takes the place of ancient myth and legend in island culture. When Hawaiian King Kamehameha died in 1819, his favorite wife Ka'ahumanu became queen of the islands. Tired of the old taboos, she eliminated the traditional religion and had all the wooden tiki idols in Hawaii burned. Soon after, Christian missionaries arrived, and by 1825, she had converted and changed her name to Elizabeth.[2] When Tonga's chief Taufa'ahau converted in 1831, he adopted the name George, after King George IV of England, and shepherded the whole kingdom into worshiping as Methodists.[3] Today, nearly all Polynesians are Christian. Whole villages pack the old and lovingly kept neighborhood churches each Sunday. Women and men alike dress in their finest Western-style shirts, with a bold-patterned cloth *lava-lava* as a wrap-around over shorts. In the Cook Islands, islands like Aitutaki celebrate Gospel Day each year, commemorating the arrival of Christianity in 1821. And yet, just inside the woods near Aitutaki's big church, lies a marae.

French Polynesians attend church in the Society Islands. Many Polynesian businesses are closed on Sundays, especially in smaller towns.

The Coconut

The beautiful princess Sina bathed every day in a clear pool of mountain water where an eel god lived. As the eel swam around her, he fell in love. The all-knowing eel told Sina that disaster was coming—that very night, a terrible flood would destroy her entire village. "Sina, you can save your house and your people," the eel told her. "I will swim to your doorstep and you must cut off my head and bury it near your hut." Sina did. After the flood, a great tree grew from the eel's burial place. Its delicious fruit—the coconut—kept Sina's people strong and healthy. And every time they looked at a coconut, they saw two eyes and a nose, a reminder of the eel that saved them.

Coconuts have been an important food source for Polynesians since native people first arrived. The coconut palm grows happily on poor soil like salty, sandy beaches. Not only does the fruit stay fresh for months, it provides both coconut water to drink and coconut "meat" to eat, all in its own reusable bowl. Polynesians have found many uses for this valuable plant. The meat, or copra, can be crushed to make coconut oil for cooking and medicine. Women and men alike slather their skin with coconut oil to keep it soft and healthy. Coconut oil mixed with turmeric, a yellow spice, was often given to sick babies or to women who had just given birth. And once all the meat was removed from the shell, the remaining coconut fiber made an excellent fire starter.

Chapter Five
Sharing Stories: Language and Film

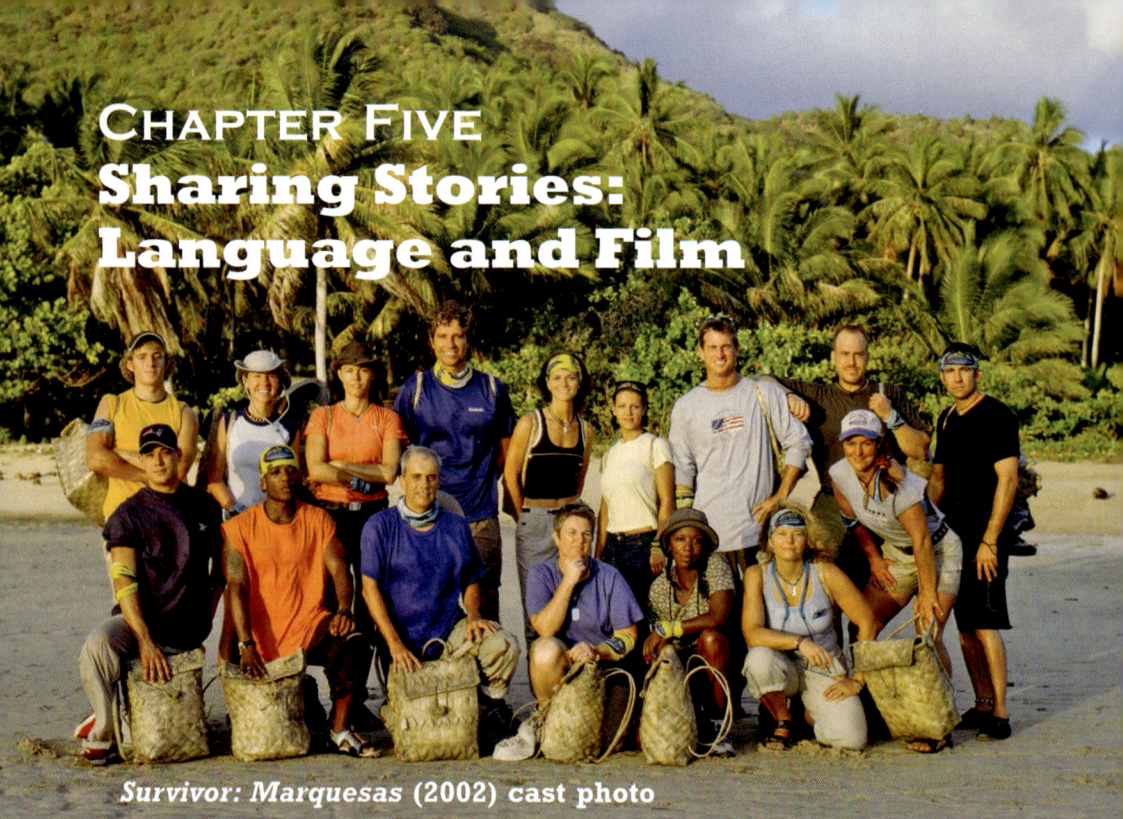

Survivor: Marquesas (2002) **cast photo**

Most Polynesians speak English, especially on islands that have a history of American or British colonization. Where France ruled, such as in French Polynesia, the official language is French. Islanders also keep at least twenty distinct Polynesian languages alive. Samoan, Tuvaluan, Tongan, and Cook Islands Maori have been made official languages of their island governments. New Zealanders include Maori as a second official language, teaching it in schools and using it on signs. Polynesian languages share many similarities, since they all evolved from the language spoken by their shared ancestors, the Lapita people.[1] English shares a few Polynesian roots, too, having adopted Polynesian words such as "taboo," "tattoo," and "ukulele."

Film and TV

The soft sand and blue waters of Polynesia first graced the big screen in the award-winning American movie musical about soldiers, colonies, and finding love, *South Pacific*, filmed on Hawaii and released in 1958. Movies like Elvis Presley's *Blue Hawaii*,

A movie poster for *South Pacific* (1958)

Chapter Five

filmed in Waikiki, continued the trend. American restaurants soon built their own wooden statues for South Pacific gods and made strong drinks bursting with tropical flavors. American pop culture went crazy for all things tiki in the 1950s and 1960s, from hula dancing and drumming to beach parties and umbrellas in tropical mai tai drinks. When the Disney World theme park first opened in 1971, it even featured the Polynesian Resort.

American TV shows, from the 1960s' TV comedy *Gilligan's Island* to the hit TV mystery *Lost* in the 2000s, popularized the idea of being a castaway in Polynesia. Contestants become real-life castaways on the popular reality show *Survivor*, which has filmed whole seasons on the Marquesas Islands in French Polynesia, on Samoa, and on the Cook Islands. Survivors race canoes, dive among coral reefs, and eat some of the same foods as Polynesians, such as the delicacy fafaru.

Chad Gates (played by singer and movie star Elvis Presley) treats his girlfriend Maile (actress Joan Blackman) to a ukulele serenade in *Blue Hawaii* (1961).

Sharing Stories: Language and Film

Now, Polynesian filmmakers are beginning to tell the story of their people. New Zealand director Niki Caro first achieved international acclaim with 2002's *Whale Rider*, based on a novel by New Zealand author Witi Ihimaera. This tale of a girl who dreams of becoming a Maori chief starred native Maori actors, including Keisha Castle-Hughes and Cliff Curtis. Castle-Hughes was nominated for an Oscar for her performance.

Whale Rider (2002) brought Maori life to the big screen thanks to a native cast and crew, including (left to right) Cliff Curtis, Niki Caro, Keisha Castle-Hughes, and Rawiri Paratene.

Aloha! Talofa! Ia Ora Na! Kia Ora! Malo e Lelei!

Here are a few easy phrases from the Polynesian languages with the greatest number of speakers.[2] Vowels generally sound the same between the islands, and are pronounced a ("ah" or "uh"), e ("eh" or "ay"), i ("ee" or "ih"), o ("oh" or "aw"), and u ("oo"). Different languages often substitute one consonant sound for another. For example, Samoans call their homeland *Savai'i* (sah-VYE-ee), while Hawaiians say *Hawai'i* (ha-WYE-ee). The Maori of New Zealand say *Hawaiki* (ha-WYE-kee), and Cook Islanders say *Avaiki* (ah-VYE-kee). An apostrophe written in Polynesian words indicates a glottal stop—a tiny spoken pause, like the one between the spoken words "uh-oh."

	Samoan	Hawaiian	Tahitian	Maori	Tongan
Hello!	*Talofa!*	*Aloha!*	*Ia ora na!*	*Kia ora!*	*Malo e lelei!*
Goodbye.	*Tofa.*	*Aloha 'oe.*	*Parahi.*	*Hei kona ra.*	*'Alu a.*
How are you?	*O a mai 'oe?*	*Pehea 'oe?*	*Maita'i oe?*	*Kei te pehea koe?*	*Fefe hake?*
I'm well, thanks.	*Manuia fa'afetai.*	*Maika'i, mahalo.*	*Maita'i vau, mauruuru.*	*Kei te pai.*	*Sai pe malo.*
Please	*Fa'amolemole*	*E 'olu'olu*	--	*Koa*	*Kataki*
Thank you.	*Fa'afetai tele.*	*Mahalo.*	*Mauruuru roa.*	*Kia ora.*	*Malo au-pito.*
Yes	*Ioe*	*Ae*	*E*	*Ae*	*'Io*
No	*Leai*	*A'ole*	*'Aita*	*Kahore*	*Ikai*

Chapter Six
Hoʻohauʻoli: Have Fun with Music, Art, and Sports

Music and Dance

The Polynesians' greatest passion is music of all kinds. The strong Christian heritage of the islands makes church singing heartfelt and popular. Aitutaki's Ziona Tapu church choir has become world famous for its joyful and beautiful song. But Polynesians cherish their own musical heritage, too. Over the years, singers have passed down favorite *himene*, or songs, that celebrate the gods, nature and rain, warriors, and love. Musicians craft melodies on handmade instruments like the *vivo*, a nose flute made of bamboo, the *pu*, or seashell horn, and the ukulele. The thunderous drums are everyone's favorites. Easter Islanders keep the beat using *maea*, special stones chosen from the sea. To make a *keho* drum, the islander places a hollowed-out pumpkin in the bottom of a wide hole in the ground. Covering up the hole with another flat stone makes a drum that can withstand the furiously fun beats of percussion-heavy favorites.

Polynesian ancestors used dance to welcome visitors, to pray to the gods, to threaten an enemy, or to flirt. Their dancing horrified

Christian missionaries who influenced ali'i. King Pomare II of Tahiti outlawed the Tahitian *tamure* dance, and especially the dancers' skimpy clothing, in 1819. But Tahitians continued to teach their children in private until France took over and relaxed the rules against dancing. Today, Tahitians celebrate a national festival of music, song, and dance, the *Heiva I Tahiti* (*heiva* means "community meeting") each June, as they have since 1881. The most talented dancers compete for the high honor of being crowned the best dancer in the village, or even in all of French Polynesia. Male dancers wear circles of leaves or grasses around their upper arms and lower legs, moving and jumping to the music. In bikini tops and loose skirts of leaves or long grasses, female tamure dancers bounce their hips hypnotically, like flames licking from a blazing fire, as drums click, beat, and bang wildly.[1]

The award-winning Hei Tahiti dance group captivates their audience at the Heiva I Tahiti on July 7, 2013.

Chapter Six

Other Polynesian islands sway to their own dances, many of which have become internationally famous. Hawaiians use hula to honor the gods and tell stories about them. Hula dancers chant names of goddesses like Pele or Laka, making every step a part of a prayer. Fire dancing originated in Samoa, first made famous by Samoan Freddie Letuli in movies and American TV shows in the 1950s. Male warrior-dancers demonstrated their skills through the ʻailao, a dance of swinging, twirling, tossing, and catching a highly decorated war club or a long knife. At night, dancers traded their weapons for lit torches to put on an acrobatic show. New Zealand Maori pride themselves on their war dance. The haka, or "fire breath," strikes fear into the hearts of enemies. Haka dancers wear fierce expressions—wide eyes, flared nostrils, and stuck-out tongues—as if they mean to devour their enemies. They chant, stomp the ground, and slap their skin. The New Zealand national rugby team, the All Blacks, performs the haka on the field before every match.

New Zealand's beloved national rugby team, the All Blacks, performs the Maori haka war dance before facing off against Australia on August 24, 2013.

Ho'ohau'oli: Have Fun with Music, Art, and Sports

Arts

Polynesian craftsmen work with the nature around them to turn useful objects into works of art. Fishermen make ornate fishhooks from bones and shimmering shells. Wood and stone carvers whittle materials into jewelry, dishes, or statues that honor their ancestors' gods like tiki or the Easter Island moai. But artisans especially show their skill through work with cloth. In a matter of minutes, skilled weavers can create baskets, plates, or hats using only coconut palm tree leaves.[2] Finer mats are made from tree bark or from leaves of the pandanus plant. A mat called the *tao'vala* is still worn as a long skirt by both men and women of Tonga for weddings and funerals. Ancient craftsmen created rich, shimmering cloaks, or *'ahu'ula*, for Hawaiian kings by attaching feathers from the red *'i'iwi* bird or the black and golden *mamo* bird to a woven net.[3]

This luxurious feather 'ahu'ula cloak may have once belonged to Hawaii's Chief Kalani'opu'u (1729–1782).

Chapter Six

For nearly three thousand years, *tapa* cloth has been an essential part of Polynesian life. Tapa can be used to make nearly anything, from loincloths for men or wrap skirts for women to sails for a canoe. Tapa cloth is made from the inner bark of the paper mulberry tree. Even today, women carry on the tradition of sitting together and talking while beating the bark with wooden mallets. They beat or glue the individual pieces of tapa together to make a larger cloth, then set out the thinned sheets to dry in the sun. The cloth can now be decorated in geometric patterns using natural dyes. To make tapa was a sign of a strong village, one that could work together. In Tahiti, a chief's status was tied to the size of his storehouse of tapa. Though most Polynesians wear modern imported fabrics, like cotton, in their everyday clothing, they treasure beautiful tapa curtains, rugs, or wall art. Couples wear tapa in their weddings, drape tapa blankets over funeral caskets, or give tapa as gifts at important family celebrations. In Tonga, families consider their tapa supply as part of their *koloa*, or wealth.[4]

To Polynesian artists, simple lines drawn into intricate patterns gave a tapa cloth special, spiritual powers. Polynesians' bodies, too, became a sacred canvas. Though Polynesians did not invent body art, their widespread practice of it gave us the word "tattoo." As the legend goes, Tohu, the Tahitian god of tattoo, painted all the fish in the ocean with beautiful patterns. The results pleased him so much that he commanded his people to decorate themselves, too.

Tapa cloth

Ho'ohau'oli: Have Fun with Music, Art, and Sports

Traditional Polynesian tattoos use needle-sharp combs made from bone and shell to pierce the skin with natural dyes, like the soot from burnt candlenuts. Polynesian warriors covered their bodies—even their eyelids and tongues—with raised tattoos to make a fierce display.[5] But ordinary men and women, too, used tattoos to display their status in society, or simply to show that they had been blessed by the gods.

Sports and Festivals

Polynesians play common world sports, like soccer and volleyball. The large, muscular Polynesian body type that once made strong warriors is famous today in international sports, especially football and rugby. NFL superstars Troy Polamalu and Haloti Ngata were both born in California, but their families hail from American Samoa and Tonga, respectively.

Creative Polynesians have invented their own sports, also. Canoe races were a natural start. Outrigger canoe clubs throughout Polynesia have spread a love of paddling to the United States and even around the world. If a canoe broke, ancient Polynesians could still make it work—as a surfboard. Surfers today seek out killer waves all over Polynesia, like the ones at Oahu's North Shore. Others just enjoy watching pros ripping the surf at locations like Teahupo'o in Tahiti at the annual the Billabong World Championship Tour. For the ultimate in thrills, Polynesians and tourists alike seek out New Zealand's picture-perfect bridges for world-class bungee jumping.[6]

Around the time that ancient Greeks organized the first Olympic games, ancient Polynesians were already participating in community festivals that centered around their love of sport. Easter Island's Tapati Festival is a modern-day version, an annual celebration of Rapa Nui sport and culture.[7] During the day, the festival hosts canoe races as well as contests of strength and skill. The *haka pei* draws fun-loving crowds to a race where men sled downhill at breakneck speed on trunks of banana trees! Even the non-athletic show a fierce competitive spirit. Family cooks present their best dishes to food judges, and the winner takes home bragging rights

Chapter Six

for the rest of the year. Master artisans display their handmade arts and crafts for sale—and even hold a mat-weaving competition. Perhaps one of the most anticipated events is the *kai-kai*, the string-figure contest. Islanders use their fingers to weave loose pictures out of string—but they also have to tell a story that brings their string figures to life in the minds of the audience. The night brings a show of grass-skirted dancers performing the *sau-sau*, whirling and swaying to the rhythm of ancient drums beneath the stars.

In 1988, AJ Hackett and Henry van Asch opened the world's first bungee-jumping business on the Kawarau Bridge in Queenstown, New Zealand. To date, over one million visitors have taken the plunge.

Recipe: Po'e (Tahitian Fruit and Coconut Custard)

Polynesians prepare this rich dessert in banana leaves and bake it in a fire pit.

Ingredients
4 to 6 servings
6 to 8 ripe bananas,* peeled and diced
½ c brown sugar
1 c cornstarch
2 tsp vanilla
1 c coconut cream**

Instructions
1. Preheat oven to 375°F and grease a 2-quart baking dish.
2. **With an adult's help**, puree the bananas one by one in a blender or food processor. Add bananas until you have 4 cups of fruit puree.
3. Add the brown sugar, cornstarch, and vanilla. Puree again until lumps are gone.
4. Pour the puree into the baking dish. Bake in the preheated oven for 30-45 minutes, until custard is firm and bubbling. Remove from oven and cool to room temperature. Cover cooled dish with plastic wrap and refrigerate until chilled.
5. Cut into cubes and serve in a bowl. Garnish with a dollop of coconut cream and a sprinkling of brown sugar.

* You can substitute just about any tropical fruit to make the puree, such as papaya, mango, or pineapple. You will need 4 cups of fruit puree for this recipe. For juicier fruits, add ¼ c more cornstarch to get the right consistency.

** Coconut cream is found at the top of a can of full-fat coconut milk that has not been shaken recently. Just open the can and scoop the cream off the top.

Experiencing Polynesian Culture in the United States

EXPERIENCE
Pacific Islander Festival—San Diego, California
This weekend festival in September features colorful dancing, live music with traditional instruments, and a cultural village with displays of traditional foods, medicines, and crafts. On Sunday, the festival hosts Christian worship services with favorite Polynesian religious songs and dress.
http://www.pifasandiego.com/

Polynesian Cultural Festival—Oakland Park, Florida
Members of Florida's Polynesian Culture Association hold an all-day outdoor festival every year in April to celebrate their heritage. Visitors enjoy traditional shows with hula and fire-dancing, basket-weaving demonstrations and other crafts, and delicious tropical drinks and authentic food from the South Pacific.
http://www.polynesiancultureassociation.com/Festival.html

Polynesian Resort—Disney World, Orlando, Florida
From tropical landscaping lit by tiki torch to the Nanea Volcano Pool and slide, the Polynesian Resort at Disney World recreates the feel of Polynesia. Guests can learn how to make flower leis, or enjoy a luau with authentic dancing at the Spirit of Aloha Dinner Show.
https://disneyworld.disney.go.com/resorts/polynesian-resort/

Disney World Polynesian Resort

Polynesian Cultural Center and Ali'i Luau—Laie, Hawaii
Over thirty-seven million visitors have toured the PCC since it opened in 1963. Learn how traditional Samoans made fire and cracked coconuts. Play games like *tititorea*, a Maori stick game, or Hawaiian bowling (*ulu maika*). You can even get a temporary Maori tattoo! Stay for the award-winning luau, where you will dine like an ali'i on sweet and sour pork and mahi mahi, and watch a breathtaking cultural show with traditional dance, songs, and even firewalking.
http://www.polynesianculturalcenter.com/

Lei Day Polynesian Festival—Las Vegas, Nevada
Each year at the beginning of May, The California Hotel & Casino transforms into an island paradise. Enjoy live Polynesian music and dancing all day as you check out displays of crafts and authentic South Pacific food.
http://www.tamaevaarii.org/index.htm
https://www.youtube.com/watch?v=ucStAgaijq8

Outrigger Canoe Clubs
Throughout southern California and in major US cities like Miami, FL; New York, NY; Philadelphia, PA; Dallas, TX; Seattle, WA
Most clubs welcome paddlers of any skill level to practice. Clubs hold friendly competitions and races in New Jersey, Florida, or on the West Coast.
http://www.philadelphiaoutrigger.com/index.html

TASTE
Mai-Kai—Fort Lauderdale, Florida
Owner Mireille Thornton's frequent visits to Polynesia inspire this one-of-a-kind restaurant. Enjoy authentic Polynesian tastes and an award-winning show, where performers dressed in tapa cloth and shells dance and sing to Polynesian drum rhythms. The restaurant itself even feels like a Polynesian village, right down to the thatch roof and wooden plank bridge at the entrance.
http://maikai.com/

Trader Vic's
Locations in Emeryville and Beverly Hills, CA; Portland, OR; and Atlanta, GA
Vic's serves up fire-roasted sweet pork and seafood, while its island vibe surrounds you with woven-fiber walls, tiki sculptures, and tasty tropical drinks for kids and adults.
http://tradervics.com/

SEE
Kaululehua Hawaiian Cultural Center—South San Francisco, California
This community center for Polynesians in San Francisco hosts art shows, films, live music, hula performances, an annual luau, and public hula and music lessons.
http://www.apop.net/

Bernice Pauahi Bishop Museum—Honolulu, Hawaii
The largest museum in Hawaii is world-famous for its collections of native Pacific animals and flowers, Hawaiian culture artifacts, and priceless heirlooms from the Kamehameha royal family.
http://www.bishopmuseum.org/

The Field Museum: Polynesian Collection and Maori Marae
1400 S. Lake Shore Dr., Chicago, IL 60605
http://www.fieldmuseum.org/explore/our-collections/polynesian-collections
http://www.fieldmuseum.org/happening/exhibits/maori-meeting-house-ruatepupuke-ii

Indiana University Art Museum: Polynesia
http://www.iub.edu/~iuam/online_modules/wielgus/polynesia.html

The Metropolitan Museum of Art
Polynesia and Micronesia, Gallery 353
1000 Fifth Ave., New York, NY 10028
http://www.metmuseum.org/collection/galleries/africa-oceania-and-the-americas/353

American Museum of Natural History, Margaret Mead Hall of Pacific Peoples—New York, New York
American explorer and scholar Margaret Mead inspired this gallery, which includes a Maori chief's elaborately carved *pataka*, or storage house, and the stone Easter Island moai reproduction which was featured in the movie Night at the Museum.
http://www.amnh.org/exhibitions/permanent-exhibitions/human-origins-and-cultural-halls/margaret-mead-hall-of-pacific-peoples

University of Pennsylvania Museum of Archaeology and Anthropology Oceanian Section
3260 South St., Philadelphia, PA 19104
http://www.penn.museum/about-our-collections/oceanian-section.html

The Mariners' Museum—Newport News, Virginia
Visit the exhibit on ancient Polynesian navigation in a gallery dedicated to the history of exploration.
http://ageofex.marinersmuseum.org/index.php?type=navigationtool&id=10

HEAR
New York Uke Fest—New York, New York
Ukulele players from around the world gather each year for concerts and lessons for everyone from master instrumentalists to kids who just like to strum.
http://www.nyukefest.com/

Pacific Islands Radio FM
Listen to the sounds of Oceania on this live-streaming popular music Internet station. http://www.live365.com/stations/janeresture

Map of Polynesia

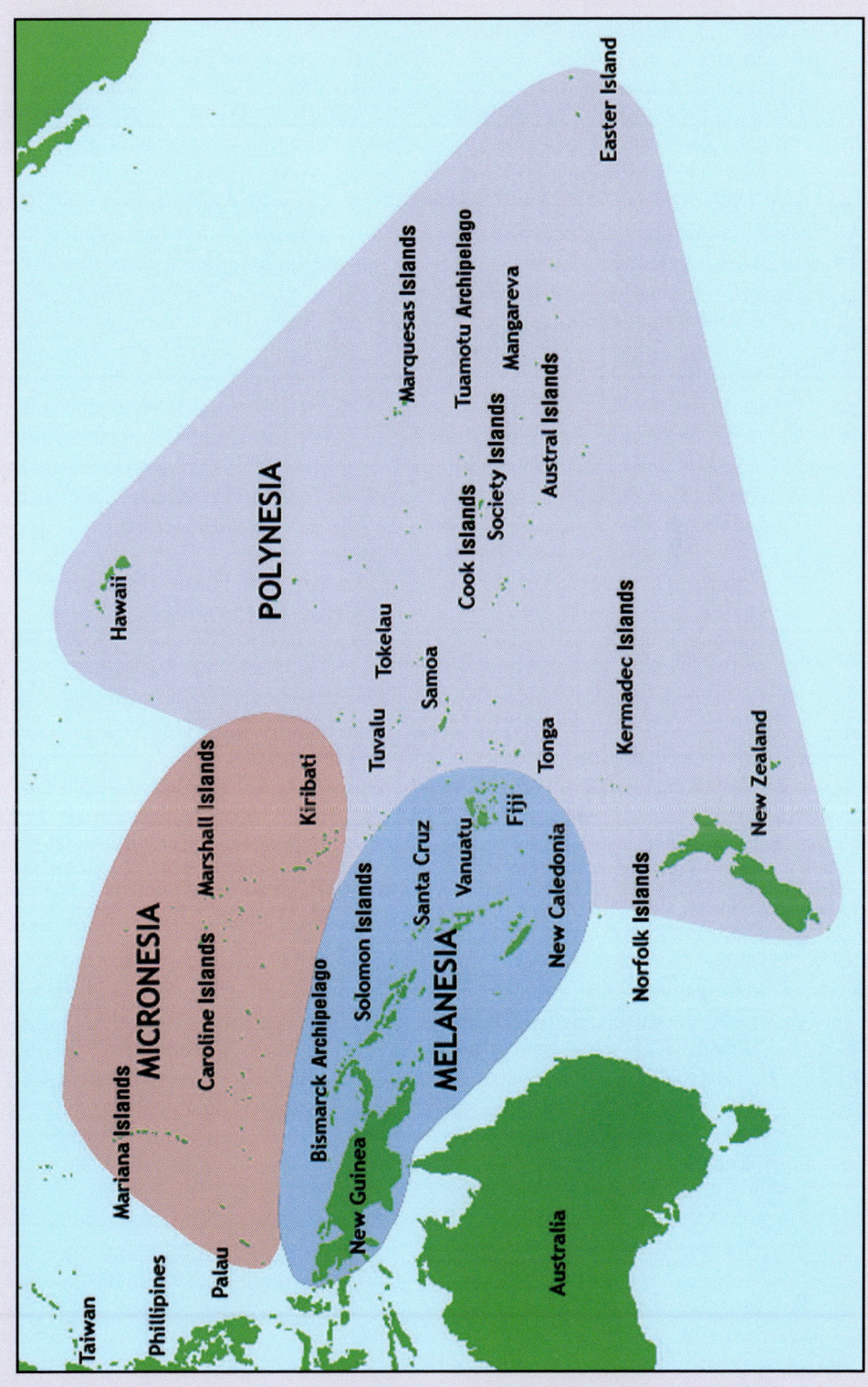

CHAPTER NOTES

Chapter 1. Where Is Polynesia?
1. Kingdom of Tonga, "True Beauty." http://www.thekingdomoftonga.com/index.php/discover/true-beauty/
2. Central Intelligence Agency, *The World Factbook.* https://www.cia.gov/library/publications/the-world-factbook/
3. Peter Bellwood, *The Polynesians: Prehistory of an Island People* (London: Thames and Hudson, 1978), p. 12.
4. Ibid., p. 13.
5. Anne Salmond, *Aphrodite's Island: The European Discovery of Tahiti* (Berkeley, CA: University of California Press, 2009), p. 465.
6. EPA, "Future Climate Change: Future Sea Level Change," March 4, 2014. http://www.epa.gov/climatechange/science/future.html#sealevel
7. Government of Tokelau, "Solar Project: The World's First Truly Renewable Nation." http://tokelau.org.nz/Solar+Project.html
8. *Matangi Tonga Online*, "Tonga's First Wind Turbine Live at Nakolo," June 18, 2013. http://matangitonga.to/2013/06/18/tongas-first-wind-turbine-live-nakolo
9. Radio Australia, *Tuvalu News*, "Tuvalu PM Vows to Continue Climate Fight," October 5, 2010. http://www.tuvaluislands.com/news/archives/2010/2010-10-05.html

Chapter 2: Hawaiki, Homeland of the Ancient Polynesians
1. Peter Bellwood, *The Polynesians: Prehistory of an Island People* (London: Thames and Hudson, 1978), p. 14.
2. Rowan McKinnon, et. al., *South Pacific* (Footscray, Australia: Lonely Planet, 2009), p. 36.
3. Richard Alleyne, *Telegraph*, "Kon-Tiki Explorer Was Partly Right—Polynesians Had South American Roots," June 17, 2011. http://www.telegraph.co.uk/science/science-news/8582150/Kon-Tiki-explorer-was-partly-right-Polynesians-had-South-American-roots.html

Chapter 3: Haole: Outsiders Come to Paradise
1. Matt K. Matsuda, *Pacific Worlds: A History of Seas, Peoples, and Cultures* (Cambridge, UK: Cambridge University Press, 2012), p. 67.
2. Donald Denoon, et. al., *The Cambridge History of the Pacific Islanders* (Cambridge, UK: Cambridge University Press, 1997), p. 124.
3. Ibid., p. 127.
4. James Siers, *Polynesia in Colour* (Wellington, NZ: A.H. & A.W. Reed, 1968), p. 6.
5. Rowan McKinnon, et. al., *South Pacific* (Footscray, Australia: Lonely Planet, 2009), p. 41-42.
6. Polynesian Cultural Center, "Samoa—The Heart of Polynesia." http://www.polynesia.com/polynesian_culture/samoa/samoa-map.html#.U3wW-PldWSo

CHAPTER NOTES

7. Carl Safina, *Eye of the Albatross: Visions of Hope and Survival* (New York: Henry Holt and Company, 2002), p. 74.
8. Donald Denoon, et. al., *The Cambridge History of the Pacific Islanders* (Cambridge, UK: Cambridge University Press, 1997), p. 325.
9. Dominique Schwartz, ABC (Australia) News Foreign Correspondent, "Ageing Rock Stars," September 24, 2013. http://www.abc.net.au/foreign/content/2013/s3855458.htm

Chapter 4: Kahiko, Tradition: Family, Food, and Faith

1. Central Intelligence Agency, *The World Factbook*, "Country Comparison: Obesity—Adult Prevalence Rate." https://www.cia.gov/library/publications/the-world-factbook/rankorder/2228rank.html
2. Donald Denoon, et. al., *The Cambridge History of the Pacific Islanders* (Cambridge, UK: Cambridge University Press, 1997), p. 194.
3. Ibid., p. 195.

Chapter 5: Sharing Stories: Language and Film

1. Matt K. Matsuda, *Pacific Worlds: A History of Seas, Peoples, and Cultures* (Cambridge, UK: Cambridge University Press, 2012), p. 19.
2. Rowan McKinnon, et. al., *South Pacific* (Footscray, Australia: Lonely Planet, 2009), pp. 302 and 498; Simon Ager, *Omniglot: The Online Encyclopedia of Writing Systems & Languages*, http://omniglot.com

Chapter 6: Ho'ohau'oli: Have Fun with Music, Art, and Sports

1. James Siers, *Polynesia in Colour* (Wellington, NZ: A.H. & A.W. Reed, 1968), p. 92.
2. Robert D. Craig, *Handbook of Polynesian Mythology* (Santa Barbara, CA: ABC-CLIO, 2004), p. 10.
3. Ibid., p. 11.
4. Rowan McKinnon, et. al. *South Pacific* (Footscray, Australia: Lonely Planet, 2009), p. 498.
5. Ibid., p. 55.
6. Steven Roger Fischer, *A History of the Pacific Islands* (New York: Palgrave, 2002), p. 278.
7. Rowan McKinnon, et. al. *South Pacific* (Footscray, Australia: Lonely Planet, 2009), p. 81.

Photo Credits: All design elements from Thinkstock/Sharon Beck; Cover—pp. 1, 13, 14–15, 16, 17, 26, 27, 30–31, 35, 36, 38, 39, 46, 53—Thinkstock; p. 3—Sri Rusden/Newscom; pp. 6–7, 8, 19, 22, 23, 24, 25, 28, 33, 49, 50, 52, 54, 57—cc-by-sa; p. 10—Design Pics/Greg Vaughn/Newscom; p. 11—Sergi Reboredo/picture alliance/Newscom; p. 12—Gregory Boissy/AFP/Getty Images; pp. 20–21—STRINGER/AFP/Newscom; p. 32—Douglas Peebles/DanitaDelimont.com "Danita Delimont Photography"/Newscom; p. 34—Los Angeles Daily News/ZUMAPRESS/Newscom; p. 37—Benali Remi/ZUMAPRESS/Newscom; p. 40—Monty Brinton/CBS Photo Archive/Getty Images; p. 41—20TH CENTURY FOX/Album/Newscom; p. 42—PARAMOUNT PICTURES/Album/Newscom; p. 43—J. Vespa/WireImage/Getty Images; pp. 44–45—Sergi Reboredo/ZUMA Press/Newscom; p. 47—Gregory Boissy/AFP/Getty Images/Newscom; p. 48—Marty Melville/AFP/Getty Images/Newscom.

FURTHER READING

Books
Bankston, John. *Margaret Mead: Pioneer of Social Anthropology*. Berkeley Heights, NJ: Enslow Publishers, 2006.
Bligh, William. *Mutiny on the Bounty*. Mineola, NY: Dover Publications, 2009.
Ngcheog-lum, Roseline. *Cultures of the World: Tahiti*. Tarrytown, NY: Benchmark, 2007.
Sperry, Armstrong. *Call It Courage*. New York: Simon & Schuster, 2008.
Webster, Christine. *Polynesians*. New York: Weigl Publishers Inc., 2012.

Movies
Caro, Niki. *Whale Rider*. Santa Monica, CA: Lionsgate, 2002.
Heyerdahl, Thor. *Kon-Tiki*. New York: RKO Radio Pictures, 1951.
Logan, Joshua. *South Pacific*. Beverly Hills, CA: 20th Century Fox, 1958.
Low, Stephen. *The Ultimate Wave Tahiti*. Chatsworth, CA: Image Entertainment, 2011.
Tatge, Catherine. *Dances of Life*. Arlington, VA: PBS Home Video, 2005.

On the Internet
American Samoa Visitors Bureau
    http://www.americansamoa.travel/
Cook Islands Tourism
    http://www.cookislands.travel/usa
Easter Island Tourism
    http://www.easterislandtourism.com/
Government of Tokelau
    http://www.tokelau.org.nz/
Kingdom of Tonga
    http://www.thekingdomoftonga.com/
National Geographic: "Tuamotus"
    http://video.nationalgeographic.com/video/frenchpolynesia_tuamotus
Niue Tourism
    http://www.niueisland.com/
Notes from Sea Level: "The Dangerous Archipelago: Losing Culture"
    http://www.jonbowermaster.com/videoplayer/videoplayer.php?videoid=1004
Pitcairn Islands Tourism
    http://visitpitcairn.gov.pn/
Samoa Tourism Authority
    http://www.samoa.travel/
Tahiti Tourism
    http://www.tahiti-tourisme.com/
Tuvalu: Timeless
    http://www.timelesstuvalu.com/

Works Consulted
Ager, Simon. *Omniglot: The Online Encyclopedia of Writing Systems & Languages*.
    http://omniglot.com/
Allen, Leslie. "Will Tuvalu Disappear Beneath the Sea?" *Smithsonian Magazine*, August 2004. http://www.smithsonianmag.com/travel/will-tuvalu-disappear-beneath-the-sea-180940704/?all
Alleyne, Richard. "Kon-Tiki Explorer Was Partly Right—Polynesians Had South American Roots." *Telegraph*, June 17, 2011. http://www.telegraph.co.uk/science/science-news/8582150/Kon-Tiki-explorer-was-partly-right-Polynesians-had-South-American-roots.html

FURTHER READING

Bellwood, Peter. *The Polynesians: Prehistory of an Island People.* London: Thames and Hudson, 1978.
Central Intelligence Agency. *The World Factbook.* https://www.cia.gov/library/publications/the-world-factbook/
Central Intelligence Agency. *The World Factbook.* "Country Comparison: Obesity—Adult Prevalence Rate." https://www.cia.gov/library/publications/the-world-factbook/rankorder/2228rank.html
Clark, Liesl. "Polynesia's Genius Navigators." PBS, *Nova*, February 15, 2000. http://www.pbs.org/wgbh/nova/ancient/polynesia-genius-navigators.html
Craig, Robert D. *Handbook of Polynesian Mythology.* Santa Barbara, CA: ABC-CLIO, 2004.
Denoon, Donald, et. al. *The Cambridge History of the Pacific Islanders.* Cambridge, UK: Cambridge University Press, 1997.
EPA. "Future Climate Change: Future Sea Level Change." March 4, 2014. http://www.epa.gov/climatechange/science/future.html#sealevel
Fischer, Steven Roger. *A History of the Pacific Islands.* New York: Palgrave, 2002.
Goodwin, Bill. *Frommer's Tahiti & French Polynesia.* Hoboken, NJ: Wiley Publishing, 2007.
Government of Tokelau. http://tokelau.org.nz/
Government of Tokelau. "Solar Project: The World's First Truly Renewable Nation." http://tokelau.org.nz/Solar+Project.html
Harvey, Brad. "Po'e." *Whats4Eats.* http://www.whats4eats.com/desserts/poe-recipe
Kingdom of Tonga. "True Beauty." http://www.thekingdomoftonga.com/index.php/discover/true-beauty/
Linden, Eugene. *The Ragged Edge of the World: Encounters at the Frontier Where Modernity, Wildlands and Indigenous Peoples Meet.* New York: Viking Press, 2011.
Losch, Kealalokahi. *Skin Stories: The Art and Culture of Polynesian Tattoo.* "Role of Tattoo." PBS. http://www.pbs.org/skinstories/culture/
Matangi Tonga Online. "Tonga's First Wind Turbine Live at Nakolo." June 18, 2013. http://matangitonga.to/2013/06/18/tongas-first-wind-turbine-live-nakolo
Matsuda, Matt K. *Pacific Worlds: A History of Seas, Peoples, and Cultures.* Cambridge, UK: Cambridge University Press, 2012.
McKinnon, Rowan, et. al. *South Pacific.* Footscray, Australia: Lonely Planet, 2009.
Pacific Climate Change Portal. http://www.pacificclimatechange.net/
PBS. *American Aloha: Hula Beyond Hawai'i.* "Film Description." http://www.pbs.org/pov/americanaloha/film_description.php
PBS. *Wayfinders: A Pacific Odyssey.* http://www.pbs.org/wayfinders/index.html
Polynesian Cultural Center. http://www.polynesia.com/
Polynesian Cultural Center. "Samoa—The Heart of Polynesia." http://www.polynesia.com/polynesian_culture/samoa/samoa-map.html#.U3wW-PldWSo
Radio Australia. "Tuvalu PM Vows to Continue Climate Fight." *Tuvalu News*, October 5, 2010. http://www.tuvaluislands.com/news/archives/2010/2010-10-05.html
Safina, Carl. *Eye of the Albatross: Visions of Hope and Survival.* New York: Henry Holt and Company, 2002.
Salmond, Anne. *Aphrodite's Island: The European Discovery of Tahiti.* Berkeley, CA: University of California Press, 2009.
Schwartz, Dominique. "Ageing Rock Stars." ABC (Australia) News Foreign Correspondent, September 24, 2013. http://www.abc.net.au/foreign/content/2013/s3855458.htm
Siers, James. *Polynesia in Colour.* Wellington, NZ: A.H. & A.W. Reed, 1968.
Squires, Nick. "Aitutaki: Cannibal Spirit Lives On." *New Zealand Herald*, May 8, 2008. http://www.nzherald.co.nz/travel/news/article.cfm?c_id=7&objectid=10508464
Suggs, Robert C. *The Island Civilizations of Polynesia.* New York: Mentor Books, 1960.

GLOSSARY

atoll (AT-awl or uh-TAWL)—a ring-shaped island formed by a coral reef.
breadfruit (BRED-froot)—a football-sized starchy fruit native to the Pacific islands.
copra (KOP-ruh)—the white "meat" which is found inside a coconut.
cyclone (SAHY-klohn)—a large, often destructive storm with high-speed winds which move in a circular motion; cyclones occur in the southern Pacific.
lei (LEY)—a string of flowers worn around the neck or on the head.
missionary (MISH-uh-ner-ee)—a person who travels in order to bring his or her religion to new communities.
mutiny (MYOOT-in-ee)—a rebellion against a leader, especially on a ship.
outrigger canoe (OWT-rig-er kuh-NOO)—a canoe with a supporting float for added stability.
typhoon (tahy-FOON)—a cyclone that occurs in the western Pacific.

INDEX

Aitutaki (Cook Islands) 11, 37, 46
ali'i (chief) 18, 24, 27, 36, 47, 50
All Blacks (rugby team) 48
American Samoa 9, 28, 36, 51
animals 6, 11, 13, 14, 16–17, 18, 26, 27, 32–33, 49
Aristotle 22
arts and crafts 6, 28, 49–51, 52
atolls 9, 11–12, 14, 20, 29
Australia 6, 28, 29, 48
bananas 17, 26, 34, 53
battles/conflicts 18, 23, 24, 30
birds 16, 26, 27, 49
blackbirding 29
Bligh, William 31
Blue Hawaii 40, 42
Bounty, HMS 31
breadfruit 17, 34, 35
Britain 24–25, 28, 31, 40
bungee jumping 51, 52

bure (huts) 18
canoes 6, 8, 16, 18, 23, 25, 36, 42, 50, 51
Caro, Niki 43
Castle-Hughes, Keisha 43
Christian, Fletcher 31
Christianity 27, 29, 37, 46–47
climate 12–15, 18
climate change 14–15, 30
clothing 23, 27, 37, 47, 49–50
coconuts 6, 13, 15, 17, 24, 25, 33, 34, 35, 38, 49, 53
Cook Islands 9, 11, 14, 18, 28, 29, 36, 37, 40, 42, 44
Cook, James 24, 26, 30
coral reefs 6, 11, 14–15, 42
Curtis, Cliff 43
cyclones 12, 13
dance 6, 25, 27, 42, 46–48, 52
de Bougainville, Louis Antoine 26

de Mendaña y Neira, Álvaro 22–24
diseases 29
Disney World Polynesian Resort 42
Dolphin, HMS 25
du Fresne, Marc-Joseph Marion 24
Easter Island (Rapa Nui) 6, 9, 18, 20, 30–31, 46, 49, 51–52
education 27
explorers 6, 16–17, 18, 20, 22–26
fale (huts) 17, 19
family 6, 32
farming 9, 12–13, 14, 17, 18, 32, 34–35
film 40–42, 43, 48
fish and seafood 11, 12, 17, 18, 23, 24, 32–33, 50
food 17, 18, 20, 23, 24, 25, 26, 32–35, 36, 38, 42, 51–52, 53
France 24–25, 27, 28, 29, 40, 47

INDEX

French Polynesia 9, 11, 12, 14, 18, 20, 23, 24, 25–26, 27, 28, 29, 31, 33, 34, 35, 36, 37, 40, 42, 45, 47, 50, 51
fruits 10, 17, 26, 32, 34, 35, 53
Gauguin, Paul 28
geography 8–9
geology 9–12
Gilligan's Island 42
global warming 14–15
Hackett, AJ 52
haole (outsiders) 6, 22–31, 40–42
Hawaii 6, 9, 10, 11, 13, 14, 17, 18, 24, 26, 27, 28, 29, 32–33, 34, 35, 36, 37, 40, 42, 44, 45, 48, 49, 51
Hawaiki (home) 6, 17, 18, 44
Heyerdahl, Thor 20
history 6, 16–18, 20, 22–31
houses 17, 18
hula (dance) 6, 42, 48
human sacrifice 18, 27
Ihimaera, Witi 43
instruments 40, 42, 46
Japan 29
Johnston Atoll (Hawaii) 29
Ka'ahumanu (queen) 37
Kalani'opu'u (chief) 49
Kamehameha (king) 37
kava 24, 35
Kiribati 29, 36
Kona coffee 35
Kon-Tiki 20
language 27, 40, 44–45
Lapita (people) 16–17, 40
LeMaire, Jacob 24
Letuli, Freddie 48
Lili'uokalani (queen) 28
Lost 42
Magellan, Ferdinand 22, 23
marae (meeting houses) 36, 37
Maori (people) 24, 25, 40, 43, 44, 45, 48

Marquesas Islands (French Polynesia) 9, 11, 18, 20, 23, 27, 28, 33, 40, 42
medicine 35, 38
Melanesia 8, 29
Micronesia 8, 29
missionaries 27, 29, 37, 47
moai (statues) 30–31, 49
music 6, 25, 27, 42, 46
mythology 8, 9–10, 16, 18, 30–31, 36–37, 38, 48, 49, 50
Netherlands 24, 25, 30
New Zealand 6, 9, 13, 15, 18, 24, 25, 28, 36, 40, 43, 44, 48, 51, 52
Ngata, Haloti 51
Niue 9, 11, 14, 28, 29
Norway 20
nuclear weapons 29
obesity 36
outrigger canoes 18, 51
Pacific Ocean 6, 8, 9, 10, 11, 17, 20
Papua New Guinea 16
Peru 20, 23, 29
pig/pork 17, 25, 32, 34
Pitcairn Islands 9, 11, 31
plants 17, 32–35
Pleiades (Matari'i— constellation) 12, 13
Polamalu, Troy 51
Pomare II (king) 47
Pomare family 27, 47
Presley, Elvis 40, 42
priests 36
rainfall 12, 13, 16
religion 8, 9–10, 16, 18, 27, 29, 30–31, 36–37, 38, 46–47, 48, 49, 50
renewable energy 15
Roggeveen, Jacob 24, 30
rugby 48
Samoa 9, 10, 17, 19, 24, 26, 28, 29, 33, 35, 36, 40, 42, 44, 45, 48
Schouten, Willem 24

seasons 12–13
slave trade 29
Society Islands (French Polynesia) 9, 18, 28, 37
South America 20, 23, 29
South Pacific 40, 41
Spain 22, 24
sports 48, 51, 52
Stevenson, Robert Louis 28
surfing 51
Survivor 42
Tahiti (French Polynesia) 9, 18, 24, 25–26, 27, 28, 31, 33, 34, 35, 36, 45, 47, 50, 51, 53
tapa (cloth) 50
tapu (taboo) 18, 24, 37, 40
taro 17, 33–34
Tasman, Abel 24, 25
tattoos 6, 23, 27, 40, 50–51
Taufa'ahau (chief) 27, 37
television 42, 48
Terra Australis 22, 24
tiki 6, 27, 36, 37, 42, 49
Tokelau (New Zealand) 14–15, 28, 36
Tonga 9, 10, 14–15, 17, 24, 27, 28, 29, 35, 36, 37, 40, 45, 49, 50, 51
tourism 6, 13, 31, 34
Tuamotus (French Polynesia) 9, 11, 20, 24, 28, 29
Tuvalu 9, 14, 15, 22, 28, 29, 40
typhoons 13, 17
United States 6, 9, 28, 29, 40, 51
van Asch, Henry 52
vanilla 6, 24, 26, 34–35
volcanoes 6, 9–11, 16
Wallis, Samuel 25
water (fresh) 9, 12, 13, 14, 17
Whale Rider 43
World War II 29, 40–41

About the Author

Claire O'Neal has written over two dozen books for Mitchell Lane, including *We Visit Yemen*, *We Visit Iraq*, and *We Visit Libya*. She holds degrees in English and Biology from Indiana University, and a PhD in Chemistry from the University of Washington. Claire loves to travel, and internationally has visited Great Britain and New Zealand. She lives in Delaware with her husband and two young boys while dreaming up her next globetrotting adventure.